Disney · PIXAR

THE INCREDIBLES

THE ADVENTURES OF
VIOLET & DASH

Friend
or
Foe?

By
Sheila Sweeny Higginson

Illustrated by
Melissa Ford and Shiho Tilley

Random House 🏠 New York

Published in the United States by Random House Children's Books, a division of
Penguin Random House LLC, 1745 Broadway, New York, NY 10019, and in Canada by
Penguin Random House Canada Limited, Toronto, in conjunction with Disney Enterprises, Inc.
Random House and the colophon are registered trademarks of Penguin Random House LLC.

rhcbooks.com

ISBN 978-0-7364-3861-2 (trade) — ISBN 978-0-7364-8263-9 (lib. bdg.)

Printed in the United States of America

10 9 8 7 6 5 4 3 2 1

CHAPTER 1
VIOLET

~~Dear Diary,~~

~~My Journal,~~

To my future self—

    Ugh, Mom, why did you even give me this journal???

    It's not like I'm going to ever be an actual writer or anything.

    I don't know what to say or where to start.

    It was a dark and stormy night?

    Call me Violet?

    Middle school: It was the best of times—NOT?

    Writing is clearly not one of my Super powers.
So how about this . . .

Hey there, Diary.

I'm Violet Parr, and I'm not like the other kids at Western View Junior High. My family is not like a lot of other families either. You might say we're special. Not exactly special—more like different.

SUPER different.

Do I look different? Because some days when I wake up and look in the mirror, I can almost forget how different I am. I just see Vi, the kind of girl who wants to go to the movies and buy the popcorn and hang out with friends.

I'm sure most of the kids I know would say I'm crazy for even thinking that. They'd LOVE to have the powers I have—being able to create force fields and turn invisible whenever I want. Or maybe they'd rather be Super-speedy, like my brother Dash. I can understand that. Truth is, being a Super has brought the Parr family a lot of drama. Piles and heaps and mountains of drama. Sure, it's also brought us closer together. It's just sometimes hard to know if it's all worth it.

Mom says my secret identity is my most valuable possession. But how can that be when my friends don't know my true self? They can't. I won't risk having more friends getting their memories erased because they've seen my powers. I was so upset when Tony Rydinger (the boy I like) didn't remember me at all. He saw me without my mask, so Mom and Dad's friend from the National Supers Agency zapped him with a memory wipe. And just like that—he didn't even remember meeting me. It's one thing to feel invisible and to feel like people don't see you, but it's a whole other world of sadness to know you've been erased from someone's life.

Mom also says doubt is a luxury we can't afford. (She'd be so proud that I'm quoting her in my diary, so I can't <u>ever</u> let her see this.) I'm having a hard time with that one, though. I still have tons of doubt. What if I could

be open about who I am and show my friends my true self without having to worry about all the mind-erase stuff? Would they still like me?

Or would they turn against me, the way people turned against my mom and dad and the other Supers for so many years? I'm worried that they'd think being a Super is a bad thing. Or even worse, that they'd be scared of me. I'm not sure how they could ever treat me the same way again.

I think things are going to have to be the way they've always been: a Super secret. It will just make life—and friendships—a lot less complicated if I keep my powers hidden. I hope it won't stop me from finding a real friend . . . someone who really knows me.

YUCK!

It's like you're puking feelings all over these pages. Who has time for feelings when there's so much to <u>DO</u>? Just be <u>SUPER</u>, already! There are bad guys to fight. Stop whining!

YOU LITTLE CREEP!

I see you've met my sneaking, snooping, irritating little brother Dash. As you can imagine, I was not so happy to see that he had stolen my diary and read it. Okay, I was beyond furious.

Dash has a special talent for getting on my nerves in a way that only a little brother can. Ugh! My blood still boils when I think about the time that he speed-crawled through the block castle I had spent all day building for my favorite doll, Princess Pamela. I thought Dad would scold Dash, but instead he was so proud of his little Super baby speedster that he nearly knocked over the table in his excitement. Nice, Dad. Forget about all the time and effort your daughter put into building her masterpiece. <u>Great parenting.</u>

Needless to say, this wasn't the first, or second, or millionth time Dash had infuriated me. And it's not easy to catch him—the little prankster does have Super speed! But if you've known him as long as I have, you know how to set a trap. Which is exactly what I did.

I grabbed the candle I got as a Secret Santa present last year—the one that smells like freshly baked cookies. Then I snuck down the hallway and lit it outside his room, leaving a scent trail as I crept to the kitchen with it. I waited behind the counter until I heard him open his door.

I knew I probably wouldn't be able to see him whirl in and out of the kitchen in search of freshly baked cookies, so I used my sibling sense (okay, I know that's not actually one of my powers, but I know my brother well). As soon as he entered the kitchen, I tossed up a force-field bubble—and trapped him in it.

You should have seen his face—he was so confused!

"What are you doing, Vi? Where are the cookies?" he asked.

"There are no cookies!" I hissed.

"Only sneaky little brothers who read their sister's private thoughts!"

"So what?" Dash replied. "They were dumb anyway.

'Waaaahhh-waaaahhh-waaaahhh, Tony Rydinger.

Waaaaahhhh-waaaahhh-waaaaahhhh, will I ever have a friend?'"

Dash got me SO FIRED UP that a surge of energy left my body and powered the force field. He definitely got a good zap, but he deserved it for invading my privacy and not even apologizing.

Dash sped around inside my force field, trying to bust his way out. He pounded his fists against it, and I laughed. He pounded his fists harder. It didn't matter. I wasn't going to let him get away . . . not until he apologized. Dash kept pounding and I kept laughing, and I could tell he was getting just as mad as I was. <u>Good!</u>

Then Jack-Jack floated over the force field, clapping his hands and giggling at Dash.

Our family wasn't sure for a while if Jack-Jack had powers. But then all of a sudden, he started doing stuff, like, you know . . .

shooting
laser beams
out of his eyes,

disappearing
into other dimensions,

and all kinds of other
crazy stuff.

Now Jack-Jack uses his powers all the time, which can be very chaotic. It's hard to predict what will happen when he comes around . . . and that was definitely the case here. This was how it started.

Me: Jack-Jack, I think I heard Mommy come in.

Dash: That wasn't Mommy, Jack-Jack. Vi just doesn't want you to play with us.

(Jack-Jack looked at me all sad and adorable. I couldn't believe it. Dash was trying to turn our baby brother against me!)

Me: That's not true, Jack-Jack! We're not playing. Dash has been naughty—so he's in a time-out.

(Jack-Jack gave Dash his best sad baby face. HA! Two can play at this game, Dash.)

Dash: Jack-Jack, Vi's not punishing me. It's a game! Want to play? Show Vi what you can do.

Jack-Jack looked at me and shot laser beams out of his eyes. I grabbed a pot to deflect the beams and they shifted to the sink, causing the water in it to boil. Of course, it took my attention away from the force field, so Dash escaped.

Jack-Jack laughed and clapped his hands. I went to pick him up, but Dash zipped past and sent me flying off my feet. Jack-Jack laughed even more.

Dash rushed around the kitchen like a tornado, knocking things over. I tried to block his path or trap him in another force field but kept missing. (My powers may have damaged a few things around the kitchen, too, but let's be honest—it was mostly Dash's fault.) Jack-Jack laughed and clapped the whole time.

That was when things got a little scary.

Dash raced past the fridge, and when I tried to catch him, I missed. Instead, one of my force fields tipped the fridge over and it started to fall—right toward Jack-Jack! Luckily, Dash rushed in and scooped him up in the nick of time.

"What are you doing, Vi?" yelled Dash. "You almost killed both of us—all because I read your stupid diary?"

"It's your fault!" I shouted. "Wouldn't you be upset if someone read your diary? And you haven't even apologized."

"I'm sorry for reading your stupid diary, okay?" replied Dash.

I was hesitant, but being the bigger person, I accepted his apology. Then we looked around the kitchen. It looked like the Underminer had plowed through it.

"What are we going to tell Mom and Dad?" moaned Dash.

We looked over at Jack-Jack, who was sitting in the middle of the chocolate cake Dad had baked the day before, tossing handfuls of it into the air and laughing.

I suggested that we blame it on Jack-Jack, but the baby wasn't a fan of that idea. He flamed up and burned the cake to a crisp.

Dash was really nervous. He thought Mom and Dad would blame him, for sure. Mom was still mad at him for breaking her favorite vase when he ran to get the mail the other day. I reminded him that the only reason he was worried about the mail was because he was expecting another letter from school. Dash had gotten in trouble during Mr. Kropp's class again. Dash said I wasn't being helpful.

"I'm doomed. Totally doomed!" he whined.

Then I had a brilliant idea. "We have to work as a team to make sure Mom and Dad don't see this mess. Like you said, just be Super, already."

"Thanks, Vi," Dash said. "I promise I'll make it up to you."

(I'll believe that when I see it.)

When you have to get things done quickly, it's good to have a little brother who has Super speed. Dash and I got almost everything cleaned up in under ten minutes. And believe me, that was like gold-medal, record-breaking time, considering the mess we made.

We decided that we would both apologize to Dad for eating all his cake. We knew he'd be okay with that if we told him we couldn't help ourselves because it was so delicious.

World's Best Super Sis

Don't get mad. . . . I just wanted to say that I'm sorry I called your diary stupid. And I'm sorry I read your diary—again. You really need to find a better hiding place. Thanks for your help earlier!

It might sound crazy, but it's kind of nice having Dash to talk to here. Mom gave me this diary, but she also likes to remind me that "sharing is caring." So maybe we can both write about our adventures in this book—if we ever have any.

Are you in, Dash? I know you're going to read this (you're not fooling me!).

YUCK!

CHAPTER 2
DASH

1. Just because I'm writing in this book, it doesn't mean I'm in. This is just a <u>test</u>. That's all it is. Who am I writing to, anyway? I'm not calling this thing Diary. Violet said I could call it whatever I want, so maybe I'll give it a cool name, like . . . Ace.

2. Ace, I am not going to write about feelings, or secret crushes, or anything like that. I am Dash Parr, man of speed and action. That's what I want to write about. Speed . . . action . . . battles . . . Super stuff like that.

Speaking of action and Super stuff, what's up with Mom and Dad? In the living room last night, they were all

"Way to go, honey!"
and
"Your strength is so impressive."
and
"I love it when you stretch your neck like that."

UGH, <u>GROSS</u>. And also, what were they thinking, going out to fight bad guys without us? I thought we were supposed to be a Super family. F-A-M-I-L-Y.

I don't care that Mom says she doesn't want us fighting crime on school nights.

I don't care that Dad said it was just a little petty larceny and they can handle it on their own.

If there's crime around to fight, no matter how petty, we should all be there.

Together.

Especially me.

I haven't had a chance to put my speed to the test in a while. Who knows how awesome I could be if I got to use my Super powers any time I wanted? Best Super ever, maybe. But if Mom and Dad have their way, we'll never know!

And if it was just a little crime, they could have let me try to handle it on my own. I'm getting older, and faster, and better—at everything! And they still don't even trust me. Fighting crime as a family is great, but why do Bob and Helen get to have all the fun? Why do they get to be the team leaders? Like, I know they're our parents, but why are they always telling us what to do? And when to do it? Why do they get to decide who does what??

Bob and Helen?

Wait until Mom hears that! You're going to get some Elasti-mom discipline for sure!

Yeah, yeah, yeah, what else is new? Dash Parr is in trouble again. Dash Parr should be FIGHTING trouble. ALL THE TIME. That's what Mom needs to see. No one can fight crime faster than me. The world needs more Dash Parr—not more Dash Parr doing boring math problems. Why do we even need fractions AND decimals? Can't we just stick with one or the other? I don't get the point.

ALGEBRA

Not for Real World Use

All this school stuff—it just gets in the way of stopping the bad guys. And where are all the bad guys, anyway? Maybe that's something we should look into. There don't seem to be as many bad guys around as there used to be, if you believe all the stories Mom, Dad, and Lucius always tell us. So what are all those villains doing? Maybe they're out there right now plotting some giant evil plan together.

Imagine what I could do if I unleashed my powers. Just picture it.

TOP 10 WAYS DASH PARR COULD SAVE THE WORLD
(if his parents would let him)

1. Speed to a small fire to stop it before it gets out of control.
2. Quickly pile up sandbags to stop a town from flooding.
3. Rush to someone who's been bitten by a poisonous snake to give them the antidote before they die.
4. In seconds, run from house to house to warn everyone about an incoming meteor.
5. Race around to make a tornado that can suck up evil alien invaders.
6. When all the aliens are gone, run around a tornado in the opposite direction to stop it.
7. Sprint to a landslide site and secure a giant net to stop the slide.
8. Deactivate a bomb and take it far away from people.
9. Create a whirlpool around a school of rabid sharks.
10. Get to the bad guys before anyone else—

DUH!

TOP 10 WAYS DASH PARR COULD GET HURT TRYING TO SAVE THE WORLD BY HIMSELF

1. Get caught in a fire—ALONE—because fire is unpredictable.

2. Get trapped under the weight of a sandbag—because you're not Super-STRONG.

3. Use all the antidote you have to save someone—then get bitten by the snake yourself.

4. Not have the math skills you need to figure out the trajectory of the meteor's path, and get hit by it.

5. Get teleported by evil aliens before you can stop them.

6. Create a double-vortex tornado and get trapped in it.

7. Get tangled up in the landslide net.

8. Accidentally drop the bomb while you're carrying it.

9. Sharks aren't mammals, so they can't get rabies—see why you need school?

10. Get caught by the bad guys—it's happened before!

Even if I'm not ready to save the world on my own yet, at least my life wouldn't be so boring if I could use my powers whenever I wanted. I could wake up late and still be the first to get to school. On a rainy day, I could race between raindrops and stay totally dry. I'd always be first to get to the lunch line in the cafeteria, so I'd always have cookies before they ran out.

Life would be so much better if I could just be my true Super self—all the time. If we could all be as Super as we really are. Then I'd even know if there are other Super kids at school. There probably aren't a lot of us, but still, it would AWESOME to have a Super friend.

Like maybe George isn't just the kid who's always farting. Maybe he's a Super with explosive gas powers! That would make science lab a lot more fun!

Or what if Mariah, the girl who's always giggling, has the power to tickle people by looking at them? Mr. Kropp's class would be SO much better if he just busted out laughing while he was teaching us.

I bet Jasmine is a Super. She looks like she can hypnotize people by staring into their soul when they talk to her.

I guess I'll never know, though, since Mom and Dad said we still have to stay hidden. And what Helen and Bob say goes for everyone in the Parr family. _Not fair!_

Still, what happens in the Parr house stays in the Parr house. . . .

Vi: BASEMENT, 6 A.M.

BE THERE!

CHAPTER *3*
VIOLET

Diary, I wish I'd known what Dash had planned for the basement at six o'clock this morning. I'd have been better prepared, or, better yet, I'd have just stayed in bed. I definitely would have at LEAST brushed my teeth first.

I trudged downstairs, barely able to see what was in front of me because my eyes were still half shut. Have I mentioned that I'm not really a morning person? Of course, Dash is always the <u>quickest</u> to wake up. No surprise there. The surprise was that he had already created a vortex of wind by racing around the basement, so when I opened the door, it was like being smacked in the face by a tornado. I was knocked off my feet.

Dash apologized for scaring his one and only

No one can ever predict THE DASH.

sister half to death at the crack of dawn. But he was very excited about his new idea. "Let's team up and be crime-fighting partners!" he said enthusiastically. I had absolutely no idea what he was talking about.

"If we can't be Super outside the house whenever we want, we can practice our powers inside the house," Dash explained. "You know, help each other work on our Super skills. A secret brother-sister training session—just for us."

Maybe it was the grogginess, but I was still confused.

"Come on, Vi," Dash pleaded. "It could be fun. See, I was trying out a new vortex-effect move, and it worked on you. I think it's pretty sweet!"

I didn't want to disappoint him—he was clearly all about the training session. And I actually did want to work on my skills a bit. Not training in the way Dash meant it, though. I don't have any new tricks I want to perfect. I've just been wondering if there's a way I can gain better control of my powers. They're so connected to my feelings that after I use them, I don't have anything left. I feel totally drained.

I explained that to Dash. He said it was worth checking out—that he could tell by the way the force field jolted him every time I got angry that there was definitely some connection between my powers and my emotions. I just wasn't sure how to, you know, train that.

"I think it's mind over matter," said Dash.

"If you can control your mind and your feelings, maybe you can control your powers a little better, too."

WORDS OF WISDOM

*That was good.
I should write
a book:
Words of Wisdom
by
Dr. Dashiell R. Parr*

Dash told me to put him in a force field and he'd try to get me mad to see if I could control my powers. I finally gave in, but I told him we needed to be quiet because it was still pretty early. Mom and Dad probably wouldn't be too thrilled if we woke them up.

Then we started our "training session." I wasn't really feeling it, especially since I wasn't even fully awake yet. But Dash (being the annoying little brother he is) did his best to change that.

Me: I'm too tired, Dash. There's no way we can test out how my anger affects my powers right now.

Dash: What if I remind you about the time I knocked over Princess Pamela's tower?

(That happened so long ago that I didn't feel the teensiest bit of anger thinking about it.)

Dash: How about the time I decided to give Princess Pamela a haircut?

Me: That wasn't nice. But no, still not mad.

Dash: What if I told you that I thought Tony Rydinger is a jerk?

Me: He's not. So nope. It's not going to work, Dash. It's not like I wake up angry.

Dash zipped behind me and pulled my hair. Then he spun me around and I toppled onto an old beanbag chair. "Can't catch me, Vi!" he said as he ran around the room, sticking his tongue out.

"Oh, yeah?" I said. "Want to see?"

I tried to capture Dash in a force field, but he kept zipping by, swiping at me over and over, always just out of my reach. I could feel myself getting more frustrated each time, until he stopped in his tracks and let me capture him.

Dash said he could tell that the second force field was much stronger. I would have to learn how to control it with my mind instead of my feelings. He wanted us to keep working on it. He could be right, but I definitely don't want to get up that early every day.

Dash said we could try to train every other day . . . like that would be much better. Then we heard a thump on the basement door. It was Jack-Jack.

"Awesome!" Dash cheered. "We can work on a combination move!"

"I don't think that's such a great idea," I told him. "Jack-Jack's pretty unpredictable."

"Just for a little while?" begged Dash. "Jack-Jack doesn't have to do anything. We can just try to capture him. If we can catch <u>him</u>, we can probably catch <u>any</u> bad guy."

He had a good point. I opened the door and picked up Jack-Jack. He squealed in excitement as I placed him on the floor. Dash took his teddy bear out of a box of old toys. He started to race around the basement, zigging and zagging all over the place. Jack-Jack cheered and laughed like he was watching a circus clown. While he was distracted, I became invisible. Then I grabbed a blanket, snuck over to Jack-Jack, and dropped it on him. I thought I'd gotten him . . . but my baby brother just phased right through the blanket.

Then we heard Mom and Dad, so I scooped up Jack-Jack and met them in the kitchen. I told Mom we'd decided to play with Jack-Jack so she and Dad could sleep in a little longer.

"That was nice of you, Violet," Mom said.

"It was Dash's idea, actually," I told her.

"Really?" Mom said, surprised. "Well, I appreciate that, Dash. You're a good big brother."

Dash had a big smile on his face.

"I try,"

he said.

"It's a tough job, but someone's gotta do it."

I just got back from a long and not-so-boring day at school. I have some awesome news. Actually, it's SOMEONE awesome. Her name is Gigi, and she just started at Western View today. We have a bunch of classes together, and in our first class, Mr. Hines asked me to help her, so we sat next to each other and then ended up hanging out most of the day. Can you believe it? She wanted to hang out with <u>me.</u> Oh, and get this—her whole name is Gigi Best. Do you know what that means? She's Lucius's niece!

But she seems pretty normal, so I don't think she's a Super. She's cool. And friendly. And funny. She's already talked to more kids on her first day than I probably have all year, and she still wanted to sit with <u>me</u> at lunch. She could have sat with anyone!

She's related to Frozone? She's got to be a Super!

Oh, and I heard she's really good at sports. Coach McCartney saw her playing during gym class and said she will definitely have a spot on our basketball team. Western View hasn't even had basketball tryouts yet!

Gigi's got skills!

Super skills?

I'm just not sure why she wants to be friends with me. Maybe she feels like she has to because I helped her out. Or because Lucius is a family friend. But I totally understand if she wants to hang out with the sporty girls or the popular girls. Everyone really likes her, and it was just her first day.

I hope she wants to continue to be my friend, though. She seems great, and it has been fun being around her. She's so normal that she made me feel normal. I kind of like the way that feels.

You like being normal, Vi? Hmmm—maybe Gigi's not a Super. Maybe she's a super villain?! She might know all about you. This could be a trick to make you feel normal so she can deactivate your powers. Maybe she can even brainwash people. Who starts at a new middle school and is popular on the very first day?

Come on. That doesn't sound normal. Gigi the Evil Genius sounds more like it. Since I'm not at Western View, it's up to you to monitor her. In the meantime, I'll keep an eye on my school. . . .

CHAPTER 4
DASH

Guess what? Vi's not the only Parr with a new friend.

Don't worry, I'm not going to get all

"He's funny and great and I don't believe it— he sat with me at lunch!"

I already told you, I'm not here to write about feelings. Vi can be excited and happy with her "normal" new friend, but I bet Gigi doesn't have a rubber rat. And really, what more do you need in life than a friend with a rubber rat?

So this rubber-rat kid, his name is Chance Diaz. It's not like he's new or anything. We've seen each other around school before. Usually we just nod when we pass each other. You know, the kind of nod that says, "Hey, what's up, I don't actually know you, but I don't have a problem with you either."

Well, today I got to Mr. Kropp's class a little early. I've been trying—really trying—to do the right thing because it's nice to be on my parents' good side for once. I was just about to open the door when I saw that Mr. Kropp wasn't there, but Chance was. And that's when I saw Chance putting the rubber rat into Kropp's briefcase. Brilliant!

I waited around until some other kids arrived, and then I walked past Chance and nodded, as if things were just the same as they've always been. Except I knew they weren't. I had a partner in pranks!

Mr. Kropp entered the room and looked all over for the class attendance sheet. He flipped through a pile of papers on his desk, started to open his briefcase, and then—

BAM!

Rubber rat!

"AHHHH!" screamed Mr. Kropp as he jumped onto his chair.

The class cracked up. It was a pretty epic prank. I looked over at Chance and gave him a thumbs-up underneath my desk.

Chance shrugged at me, like he was saying, "Who, me?"

Yeah, you, Chance. That's who. It takes a prankster to know a prankster.

I held out my hand to Chance after the class. "Well played," I said.

"Thanks," he replied. "I've admired some of your pranks, too. They were ... inspiring!"

"Really?" I said. "Which ones?"

We started talking about some of our favorite Kropp pranks:

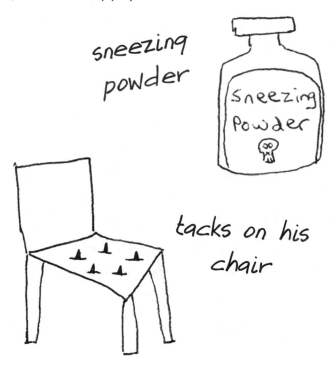

sneezing
powder

tacks on his
chair

"What's more fun than pulling pranks on Mr. Kropp?" asked Chance.

"Pretty much nothing," I said.

Even though, you know, catching bad guys is definitely more fun. But I couldn't share that.

Chance said we should plan some more pranks together. I said I was in.

This guy is
<u>AWESOME.</u>

Well, I gotta dash. I'm supposed to meet my tutor to work on my math homework.

WHO TUTORS
DURING LUNCH?
SIGH . . .

Hello, Ace (and future readers of the world—who knows, maybe I'll be famous one day). Dash Parr reporting again—and NOT from my wild imagination, as some may believe (cough—Violet—cough). Just the facts.

FACT:

When I sat down in Ms. Dermilio's room (she's the music teacher), I realized that I had gotten so wrapped up in thinking about pranks, I'd forgotten to stop at my locker to get my recorder.

"There goes my good streak,"
I thought.

"Mom will be hearing about this one."

Unless I use my super speed to make things right.

Yep, a little speed goes a long way. Come on, you'd do it, too, if you could— Ms. Dermilio is a super-strict teacher! I knew if I didn't have my instrument, she'd send a note home and I'd get a zero for the day. It was definitely worth the risk!

So here's the weird thing—Ms. Dermilio was standing at the front of the classroom, writing on the board, when I bolted out of my seat. But when I got all the way down the hall and around the corner to my locker, Ms. Dermilio was standing there talking to the principal. That didn't make any sense.

How could she be in two places at once?

I grabbed my recorder before either of them could notice, then sprinted back to class. As I got to my seat, Ms. Dermilio was walking around the room, checking to see if my classmates had the right finger position on their recorders. I pinched myself, just to make sure I hadn't fallen asleep while daydreaming or something. Nope, I was wide awake. So I tried to figure out how I could have seen what I had just seen.

My
Theories:

Almost Positively Sure—
Ms. Dermilio is a Super.

Could Be Possible—
Someone is cloning teachers,
like in a sci-fi movie. I don't
even want to _think_ about that.

Not Very Likely—
Another teacher is pulling
a prank on the principal and
wearing a very realistic mask.

Impossible—
I need glasses.

After music class, all I could think about was my double Dermilio vision. I almost spilled it to Chance when I saw him that afternoon. But we had just started hanging out, and I didn't want him to think I was crazy. Also, how could I explain how I'd gotten in and out of the class so quickly? I could tell Chance was a little disappointed that I was distracted and didn't have any new prank ideas. I apologized and said that music class had thrown me off my game.

BUT THEN ... in gym, Mr. Lannon ran into the supply room to get volleyballs for our class. I figured I'd use my Super speed to get a drink from the water fountain. But when I raced outside, I spotted Mr. Lannon in the hallway with the principal! How could he be in the hallway AND in the supply room AT THE SAME TIME?!? That can't be a coincidence. Did I see two different teacher clones on the same day???

On the way home, I thought some more about it. Maybe Ms. Dermilio and Mr. Lannon aren't Supers, but the principal is. If he could warp time, that might explain why these teachers were in two places at the same time.

Or maybe—
just maybe—
it was Gigi!

She could have snuck into my school to do some villainous stuff.

I bet
that's what
it is!

Dash Parr, please. Gigi didn't sneak into your school. She was at Western View all day. I know because I was with her. She's NORMAL. My NORMAL friend. I think you might even like her. Mom said something about inviting her over for dinner with Uncle Lucius and Honey. You'll get to meet her then. You'll see how nice she really is.

What's funny is that when I mentioned dinner to Gigi, she asked if we had plans to go skiing soon.

"Uncle Lucius really loves hitting the snowy slopes," she laughed.

And then she winked at me.

I haven't seen anything that makes me think that Gigi is anything but normal. But that did make me wonder if she knows that her uncle isn't.

I want to find out what's going on with these teachers, though. There's no way someone would risk pretending to be Ms. Dermilio—everyone knows she doesn't have a sense of humor. She'd probably get another teacher fired for that kind of prank.

But you might really need to get your eyes checked, Dash. When's the last time Mom took you to the eye doctor? Or maybe in your rush, you just thought another teacher looked like Ms. D? Then again, I guess that doesn't explain how you also saw two Mr. Lannons. . . .

It could just be your imagination running as fast as your feet again. There's probably a simple explanation for it, and you're trying to turn it into a SUPER drama.

꿇꿇꿇꿇꿇꿇꿇 꿇꿇꿇꿇꿇꿇꿇

See, I knew you would blame this on my imagination! I didn't just _think_ I saw. I definitely saw Ms. Dermilio wearing her classic G-clef sweater. No one else has a sweater like that.

I also saw Ms. Dermilio's Medusa hair. No one else has hair like that. Just to rule out every possibility, I actually went to the nurse to get my eyes checked. I told her I was having trouble seeing the blackboard. She gave me a vision test, and guess what: perfect vision!

$$Super\ boy = Super\ eyes$$

I'm telling you, Vi. There's something weird going on here. And I'm going to figure out what it is! I'm not into "drama." We know evil is out there. We've seen it. So stop trying to pretend like everything is normal when you know we're not normal.

CHAPTER 5
DASH

The CRAZIEST thing happened to me today. This is not an exaggeration. Prepare to be shocked. Prepare to be awed. Prepare to be . . . AMAZED.

This morning, when I left for school, I decided I would get to the bottom of this teacher mystery. It was a case for Detective Dash: private eye by day and Super by night. It was up to me to solve the Case of the Teacher Clones!

I was standing at the bus stop when Violet walked over. I thought it was weird because she had told me she was going to get a ride to school with Gigi.

"Oh, Gigi had to cancel," said Vi. "It's okay. I can go to the library and catch up on some homework I forgot to hand in."

Are you getting this? Violet is not the Parr who forgets to turn in homework. That would be me.

Then I started talking to her about the clones at my school—and she seemed totally surprised. She was really interested and had a million questions. Still, it was weird. I know—and you know—that Vi already read my theory about the teachers. Why would she act like she knew nothing about it? I thought maybe there really was something wrong with me.

I didn't see you this morning at the bus stop. This is getting really freaky. Who were you talking to??

The weirdest thing of all was that Violet sat with me on the bus. We NEVER sit with each other on the bus. She always says, "EWW, I'm not sitting with my little brother! That's SO uncool." And why would

I want to sit with her, anyway? It's not like she's a bright ray of sunshine in the morning (or ever).

Anyway, "Violet" sat with me and asked me a ton of questions about Chance. Like

"What do you think of him?"
and
"Have you noticed anything strange about him?"

I've only known the guy for a few days, so these seemed like really weird questions. And why would my sister be so interested in my new friend?

When I got to my stop, "Violet" got off the bus with me. I asked why she was coming to my school and not hers. She was nervous and said she was supposed to meet Gigi at my school so they can walk together. Weird, huh?

But this got me thinking. . . .

Could my sister, Violet, be . . . a clone?

Okay, I'm confused. What are you talking about? I didn't ride the bus with you this morning. Is this some kind of joke?

So now it's Detective Dash and the Case of the Teacher (and Sister) Clones!

An ordinary kid would turn down a case like this, but thankfully, I'm no ordinary kid.

What I knew:

* I met Chance Diaz.
* I saw a clone of Ms. Dermilio.
* I saw a clone of Mr. Lannon.
* I talked to a clone of Violet.

Conclusion:

All this weird stuff started happening after I met Chance.

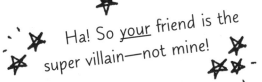

Ha! So <u>your</u> friend is the super villain—not mine!

Could Chance be a Super? I had to know for sure, so I decided to tail him. But I needed his schedule.

Before the first bell, I waited for Chance by his locker. I thought he wasn't going to show, but he came running up to me. He was all out of breath and said he "woke up late." A likely story.

I asked if I could see his schedule. I said I wanted to see if a girl I liked was in any of his classes. I told him it was a big secret. He shrugged and handed his schedule to me.

While he was unpacking his books, I scribbled down his whole schedule in my notebook. Didn't know I could write at lightning speed, too, did you?

All morning, whenever Chance and I weren't in class together, I zipped through the school to make sure he was always where he was supposed to be. And he was. There were no teacher clones either. Chance was a Super, all right—Super predictable. It's almost like he knew I would come looking for him.

I had to switch things up, so at lunch, I held my stomach.

"Oww, ahhhhh!" I groaned. "EOWWWW!!"

"What's wrong?" Chance asked.

"The pain! It's unbearable!" I gasped. "Can you walk me to the nurse? I'll have her call my dad."

It was definitely my best performance.

Chance walked me over to the nurse's office. As soon as the bell rang, he left for class, and my mysterious pains ended.

"What was it this time, Dash?" the nurse asked. "Chalk dust in your eye? Chicken pox? Pretend-itis?"

NURSE'S OFFICE

nurse is in

"I think it might have been gas," I said. I figured that was a pretty embarrassing thing to admit, so she'd think I was being honest.

I let the whole period go by, and then after the next bell rang, I snuck past the nurse and bolted down the hall. I hid behind the trophy cabinet and peeked into the science lab. Mrs. Rossi was holding up a beaker and looking very excited as she poured a blue liquid into a pitcher. Then I saw Chance leave the lab through the back door with a hall pass in his hand.

I tried to allow some distance between us, so Chance wouldn't see me if he looked over his shoulder. You know, Detective 101 kind of stuff. But when I hurried around the corner, he was nowhere in sight.

That's when I spotted Mrs. Rossi in the main office. How could she be in the lab

AND in the main office? The most obvious conclusion: TEACHER CLONES ARE REAL.

But I had to be 100% sure. I still didn't know if Chance had anything to do with it, but I was ready to confront Mrs. Rossi and see what she had to say for herself. I waited outside the office for what seemed like hours. The thing is, Mrs. Rossi never came out of the office. When the door opened, I found myself looking at . . .

MYSELF!

DASH!!! You can't leave me hanging like this! What do you mean you were looking at yourself???

CHAPTER *6*
DASH

Ace, you know my sister, Violet. She's a patient person. She might be one of the most patient people I've ever met. I don't know how she does it. Patience isn't something that comes easy to me. I always want to rush ahead at full speed.

Where were we? Right, Dash Parr looking at . . . Dash Parr. Except the other Dash wasn't me. I knew that. I just didn't know who—or what—I was looking at.

The fake Dash looked around, checking to make sure no one was watching. Then his face and body started to get all twisty and melty. It looked kind of like a bowl of ice cream after you leave it in the sun on a hot summer day. The shapes and colors started dissolving and swirling into each other. It still looked like me, a little, but it looked like someone else, too. Then it started looking less like me and more like someone else—and then not at all like me, and just like—

Chance!

I was speechless, but he was cracking up. He couldn't even talk, he was laughing so hard.

"Dash, your face . . . it was hilarious," howled Chance. "I wish you could have seen it!"

Well, I actually <u>did</u> see my face, but I didn't find it funny at the time.

Chance slapped me on the back. "Come on, Dash, you have to admit—

BEST PRANK EVER!"

Then Chance said he'd been hoping to get my attention with the teacher clones, but he had to make sure I could be trusted. I asked him how he even knew that I was a Super—before you say anything, Violet, I'm always really careful when I use my powers at school. There's no way he could have ever seen me!

▶ Yeah, sure. Then how did he know? ◀

"I heard there was another Super at this school," Chance said. "I had no idea who it was, but I needed to find out."

I asked how he knew that, but I don't think he heard me. He started talking really fast, and said that my pranks had tipped him off. He couldn't figure out how I could put things in Mr. Kropp's briefcase and in his desk so easily.

"I'm good at pranks, but you're the MASTER," Chance said. I couldn't argue with him there.

▶ Now it's _my_ turn to barf. ◀

So here's what happened:

Last week, Chance transformed into a fly (yes, a fly!) and landed on my shirt so he could tag along wherever I went.

 It would be creepy if it weren't so AWESOME.

I guess I had started zooming around the classroom and Chance went along for the ride. That was how he knew I was a Super.

I knew it! He did see you use your power. You really need to be more careful.

Chance had been worried I'd freak out if I knew he'd found out about my powers. So he started testing the waters. He transformed into different teachers to see how I would react. Then he changed into Violet to grill me with questions.

"Are you kidding?" I said. "I've been waiting to find a Super friend FOREVER!"

I bombarded Chance with questions. Can he turn into anything he wants? He thought so, but it has to be a human or an animal, and he has to at least be able to see it or look at a picture of it. Out of sight, out of shape-shifting mind.

How long can he stay transformed? He isn't sure, but it's not for very long. He's still practicing to see if he can stay in one form for a longer period of time. He gets tired easily because it takes a lot of concentration.

But still, it's SO COOL.

His parents definitely aren't Supers, and they have no idea that Chance is one. He's adopted, and he didn't know he could shape-shift until third grade! He hasn't been able to use his powers very much, so he's still trying them out. He said he's never used them to fight crime or do anything cool like that. I lied and said I hadn't fought crime yet either.

I didn't think Mom and Dad would be very happy if I shared that information.

After school, Chance showed off his Super skills in an empty classroom. Even though I think speed is a much better Super power, his ability to change shapes was pretty impressive. We actually made up a game where I showed him pictures on index cards, and Chance shape-shifted into each thing.

Anaconda—done!

Bumblebee—got it!

I wasn't about to let Chance be the only show-off in the room. I ran circles around anaconda Chance so quickly that he tied himself into a knot. Bumblebee Chance got dizzy trying to watch me run.

"Just imagine the things we can do together!" he exclaimed.

"You know what would be cool?" I said. "Fighting bad guys. Dash and Chance: the best pair of crime-fighting buddies the world has ever seen."

"Shouldn't it be Chance and Dash?" asked Chance. "You know, alphabetical order and all."

"Dash and Chance" does sound a lot better, but I wasn't going to get picky about it. I have a SUPER friend!

Yay, me!

"One more thing," Chance said. "I want to fight crime and solve mysteries. But we shouldn't let it get in the way of the real fun—SUPER PRANKS!"

I agreed.

"SUPER PRANKSTERS FOR LIFE!"

We even made up our own Super Pranksters handshake. I can't show it to you, though. It's top-secret.

Dash, I'm really happy you finally found a Super buddy. I'm still <u>very</u> weirded out that he pretended to be me, though. Please tell him never to do that again. I just think you should be careful. Remember, you've gotten in big trouble for some of your pranks. Do you think it's a good idea to team up AND supersize them? And whatever you do, don't tell Chance about the rest of the family. Our Super powers are the Parr family secret, and it's not yours to share.

CHAPTER 7
CHANCE

I told Chance I've been writing stuff down about my adventures. He thought it was a great idea, so he wrote something to add to the journal.

Don't worry,

I didn't tell him about the Parr family secret

or

let him read Ace.

He totally understood. He was just happy to be included! I really like what he wrote. You can read it here!

Hi there.

Allow me to introduce myself: Chance Diaz, at your shape-shifting service.

My good buddy Dash told me he started writing about the things he's been doing and the things that have been happening to him—one of which is me.

Most important about me, and what happens to be my biggest secret, is that I'm a Super. It's fun, but it has made me feel kind of lonely for most of my life. I don't know any other Super kids (or Super grown-ups) except Dash, and I didn't even find out about him until very recently.

I guess I always felt different from everyone else, but I didn't exactly know why. I don't even know if I've had my Super power since I was a baby. If I had it back then, I didn't know anything about it, and thankfully neither did my parents.

I remember the day I found out that I could transform myself like it was yesterday. Abuela had taken me to the library. I had taken out a big book about animals because they were my favorite thing at the time. Alone in my room, I stared at

this one picture in the book. It showed a cheetah, which I thought was the coolest animal because of its spots and speed.

Ha! That cheetah would have nothing on my speed!

I kept staring at the photo. I wondered what it would be like to prowl through the grasslands. The next thing I knew, I had paws and spots! I thought maybe I was in a dream, but everything seemed so real.

I got really worried I'd be a cheetah forever. When I imagined myself as a cheetah, I didn't want it to happen right there, in my room! Who wants to be a cheetah living in a house in the suburbs? Even worse, what would Abuela say if she saw me? She'd probably faint!

I didn't know what to do, so I closed my eyes. I just tried to relax, and soon enough, I was back to my regular Chance self.

For a long time, I was afraid to try anything like that again because I wasn't sure if I'd be able to get back to myself. Honestly, I only just started testing out my powers at the beginning of this year.

Now that I'm one half of a Super team, though, I'm ready to really see what I can do. I want to get bigger—and smaller, taller, and shorter—than ever before. If I can see it, I can become it.

Can you even guess how epic our pranks have been since we found out we're both Supers? Dash and I flew through all the classics. We placed a rubber band around the sink faucet in the teacher's lounge, and the water went everywhere! We added sneezing powder to the tissue boxes, and people can't stop sneezing! I shape-shifted into a tarantula during science class, and Dash used his Super speed to place me under Mrs. Rossi's magnifying lens. She shrieked like she was in a horror movie! (It's a good thing she doesn't have the best aim, or she would have smashed me flat! Dash whisked me away just in time.)

Classic
Pranks
101

Mr. Kropp thinks he's been put under a strange curse. I've turned into so many things that Dash has dropped into his briefcase—a frog, a stinkbug, and even a naked mole rat. I have bigger plans for us, and let me tell you, they're going to be mind-blowing!

I almost feel like a different person now that I have a friend like Dash. I don't understand why we have to hide our powers. Don't Supers have the right to be themselves wherever and whenever they want? Dash could win every race for the track team, and he should! That's not even a question!

And what's wrong with the other kids being a little afraid of us? They're not always the nicest. Steve thinks he's so tough, and that he can say whatever he wants to anybody. He told me my sneakers were trash in front of a bunch of other kids. I wonder how he'd feel if I turned into a gorilla and beat my chest in front of him. I bet he wouldn't feel so tough then. Jada made fun of Dash's hair.

She asked him if he had used a wind tunnel to style it that morning. Dash could run circles around her and show her what a wind tunnel really feels like!

If we could be ourselves—our Super selves—all the time, no one would ever dare mess with us. So I think we should reconsider keeping everything under wraps. If I were a math genius, I'd be at the top of the Principal's List. If I had musical talent, I'd be the star of the school play. Our Super skills are our talents. We need to be free. We need to show them off. We need to DOMINATE!

Your shape-shifting friend,
Chance

This guy is the best!

Gee, thanks for sharing that, Dash.

We need to dominate?

I just want to get through gym.

And I think you're starting to act weird (well, weirder than usual). You're hardly ever around anymore. It seems like you're always at Chance's house, plotting some new prank together. I'm afraid that you're going to get caught. Mom and Dad would go ballistic, especially if they suspected you're using your powers for no good. And then they'll get mad at me for not doing anything about it and for not keeping an eye on you.

Even when you're home, all you talk about is Chance. Look, it's great that you have a friend you can be yourself with. But you have a family, too. And it feels like you've forgotten all about us. You're in Super Buddy Land all day, every day.

What about Super siblings?

Wasn't that <u>your</u> idea?

SUPER NORMAL

I know I said it might be nice to have a Super friend, but having a non–Super friend is nice, too.

Life doesn't always have to be lived at top speed or filled with drama all the time. It's nice to just have someone to hang out with in a normal way, and share secrets and laugh together. I don't want you to ditch that for endless pranks. If you race down that path, I think you might be heading for trouble.

And as much as I hate to admit it, I'm worried about what might happen to you if you keep hanging out with Chance. Since we're letting friends add to this book, I have a note from Gigi that I passed to her in class:

Hey, G—quick question. Have you ever seen something happening to a friend or family member and you knew it just wasn't right? Like, if they were being influenced in a bad way. What did you do? HELP!

Hey, V, are we talking about Dash? You worry too much. From everything you've told me, your little bro is a **good kid**. He's got a great big sister for a role model. How could he not be? I'm sure he'll see the light. I mean, he's got to get tired of all those pranks sooner or later.

Hey, "V"—are you kidding me? I'm not supposed to say anything about our Super family to my friend, and you tell yours about my pranks? Like "G" said, stop worrying about me! I'm NOT a baby.

I did not call you a baby. I'm just trying to be a good big sister. I am not going to let you add stress to our lives. Whenever Mom and Dad get mad at you for doing dumb things, like pulling pranks on Mr. Kropp, they take it out on me, too. Have you ever thought of that?

If you keep doing this, I'm going to put a stop to these pranks, and your new friendship with Chance. If I need to use my powers to do it, so be it. We'll see how far you and Chance get with your pranks when there's a force field around you.

Yeah, right. Is your life really that boring, Violet? I think you're just jealous because you found a boring, normal friend who's just like your boring self. I don't know why I ever wanted to team up with you anyway. Chance is a MUCH better Super—and he'd be a better sibling, too!

GO AWAY! Leave me alone!

FINE!

Go ruin your life, for all I care.

I'm done with you—and this diary!
Just pretend you don't have a sister.
I'm sure that will make your life really

SUPER! ! ! !

CHAPTER *9*
DASH

I guess it's just us, Ace.

Can you believe what a big baby Violet is? She ran away crying.

"BOO-HOO! You're going to get us in trouble."

There's nothing to worry about. Like Chance said—it's our time to DOMINATE!

I haven't told you yet, mostly because I knew if Violet read about it, she'd really fly off the handle, but Chance has a new prank he wants us to try. We decided that as Super friends, we're going to do everything together.

Not going to lie, I've never done anything like this before. I'm not even sure I understand exactly how it's a prank. The way he first described it, it sounded—as Vi would say—like trouble. All I knew was it had something to do with sneaking into the main office after school. I told him I'd need to think about it a little more.

But you know what? Dash Parr is no baby. And I'm not going to let my sister run my life. If my Super friend wants to do it, then I say let's just be Super, already! How dangerous could it be?

As bad as Syndrome?

The Underminer?

The Screenslaver?

When duty calls, Dash answers. I'm a Parr, and we always come out on top.

I asked Chance for more details about the prank, but they weren't exactly what I'd expected. They sounded even more on the shady side than they did at first. Chance said we would sneak into the main office after school . . . and steal all the school records.

Student Records

He was so calm about it all, as though he were saying, "Then we're going to grab some popcorn before we go into the movie."

"Wait . . . what?"
I asked.

"Steal school records?"

I didn't feel good about it. "Why would we want to do that?" I asked. "I don't see how that's a prank."

"I know, it doesn't make a lot of sense if you don't know the whole plan," Chance explained. "But I can't tell you everything yet. This one is going to be good for Supers everywhere. It's really important that we do this."

"Why would a prank be good for Supers?"

I asked.

"Aren't we just doing it for fun?"

"For both,"
Chance said.

"Fun for us,
good for Supers.
You'll see. You just have
to trust me, Dash. That's
what friends do, right?
Trust each other."

"Right,"
I said.

"Just as long as no
one gets hurt."

"Who said anyone's going to get hurt?" Chance asked. "And why are you always worrying about a bunch of normal people? I think your sister is starting to rub off on you. She has you thinking like them too much. Time to face reality, Dash. Those normal kids, they're the ones holding us back from our true potential. Who cares about their little lives and problems?"

I kept thinking about what Chance said. I know he's not a bad kid. He's just obsessed with using his powers. I think it's all kind of gone to his head.

I can't help hearing Vi's voice, though. Stealing school records? That's a pretty bad thing to do, even for a prank. I don't think Chance wants to destroy the records or anything, but still, it just feels wrong. What would Mom and Dad say if we got caught? Mom might not even get mad—she might be so disappointed in me that she'd cry. That would be much worse. And what would happen to us?

It might get us into a lot more trouble than detention.

DETENTION SLIP

Name

Dash Parr

has been assigned detention.

Reason for Detention

Criminal Activity and More

Chance just wouldn't let it go, though. Every time we got together, he kept reminding me about the big prank. He said things like:

"You trust me, right, Dash?"

and

"You know I've got your back!"

and

"Are you ready for the most epic prank of all time?"

As Chance got more and more excited about the prank, I was becoming less and less convinced that it was a good idea. I started getting butterflies in my stomach every time I ran into him. Then it started feeling like I had a mob of kangaroos in there. I even ran away once when I saw Chance heading toward me in the hallway.

What am I doing? I finally found a Super friend, and now I'm running away from him.

That's crazy!

I wish I had someone to talk to. Someone who would listen, who wasn't all wrapped up in Super domination, and was kind of . . . normal. Someone like Violet.

She's still not speaking to me, though. And worse, if she knew about this plan, she'd totally freak out and probably never let me talk to Chance again. I'm not ready to give up my one and only Super friend yet—even if he does have a shady plan in mind.

I'm going to have to take a stand and do what's right. That's what Supers do. I know a lot more Supers than Chance does, and I don't think any of them would go along with this plan.

I met Chance at his locker this morning. It did not go well.

Chance was all excited about the plan. He said tomorrow would be the best day to carry it out because there was a big teacher conference. Having all those substitute teachers would make sneaking around a lot easier.

But I took a deep breath and said I wouldn't do it. And it all went downhill from there. . . .

Chance: What are you talking about? Do you
have a track meet tomorrow?

Me: I don't have anything to do tomorrow,
Chance. I'm not doing your prank.
It's not right. I can't be a part of it.

(This was when Chance got REALLY upset.)

Chance: Don't you trust me?? I thought we
were SUPER FRIENDS. We were
in this together. How can you
just ditch me?

Me: How can I trust you if I don't even
know the full plan? You won't tell me
what's going on! Why do we need the
school records? I don't want to get in
trouble for a plan that I don't know
anything about.

Chance: Since when are YOU, the amazing
Dash, afraid of getting in a little
trouble? How Super is that?

Me: Chance, I am a Super. Just because I don't want to be part of your shady plan doesn't mean I'm not a Super. It just means I'm also smart.

Chance: You're going to regret this, Dash. You just lost a friend and an opportunity to be a part of Super history.

So, like I said, it's just us, Ace. No sister. No best friend.

Did I do something wrong?

I have some bad news, Ace.

It looks like Chance did something serious. It doesn't look good. In fact, there was a police car in front of the school this morning! I've never seen a police car at school before.

The main office was buzzing. I didn't even need to see the police report to know what happened. But I wanted to talk to Chance first. It could have been something else. Maybe Mr. Kropp has a secret need for speed. Maybe he was busted doing 25 in a 20 mph zone. (Not likely.) Then I overheard Mr. Kropp and Ms. Rossi talking about the break-in. Yeah, it was the school records room. It just had to be Chance.

I wish it wasn't. I wish I could tell them it was just a prank. I wish I knew for sure that it _was_ just a prank. Most of all, I wish I could talk to Vi right now. I need to figure out what to do about Chance.

It's almost time for school, though, and I still haven't seen him around. I'll give an update later.

I'm back, Ace. Let me tell you, I wasn't sure I was going to make it. Duty called, and I answered.

After school, I had track practice. (Not that I need to practice, obviously.) Chance didn't show up at school all day. No one seemed to think anything of it, but my mind was still on him and the break-in. I just kept jogging around the track, over and over, trying to block it out of my mind.

Coach Debbie called out my name, but

I told her I would stay behind to do some extra laps. She left with the rest of my teammates, who were panting and gulping down water. I hadn't even worked up a sweat.

One lap, two laps . . . 299 laps . . . It wasn't like I was getting tired or anything. Then I heard what sounded like clapping.

It was Chance.

"Way to be . . . normal,"
he said.

"Looks like a lot of fun, jogging around out there."

"Shut up," I said. "You're lucky you're not in jail right now."

He seemed confused at first. I pointed out that stealing school records was illegal, and he shouldn't have taken them. Chance said I didn't know anything and that I should have trusted him.

"Are you trying to say you didn't do it?" I laughed. "Do I look stupid?"

"Just a little," Chance laughed. "Must be from hanging out with too many normal people."

"What is your

PROBLEM WITH NORMAL PEOPLE???"
I screamed.

"What is your

PROBLEM WITH SUPERS???"
Chance yelled back.

I had never been so angry. I ran full speed ahead—straight into Chance. He fell onto his back. Then he laughed.

"You want to battle, Parr?" he asked, pulling a pack of cards out of his back pocket.

He shuffled the cards and tapped on one of them. His face and body began to twist shape. In seconds, I was face to face with a terrifying T. rex.

ROAR!!!

I didn't even remember that I could crawl at Super speed. I don't think I've done that since I was Jack-Jack's age.

But lucky for me, I still could. Otherwise, I might have been chomped by Chance's bone-crushing teeth.

"You're such a baby!" he laughed, after transforming back to himself.

"Crawl, baby, crawl!"

"I'M...NO... BABY!!!"

I yelled as I ran toward him again. I balled up my fists and unleashed a flurry of punches—but for once, I was too slow. Chance had transformed into a rhino, so I was punching his tusk. And it hurt.

"No fair!" I shouted as I raced away from charging rhino Chance.

Chance continued to taunt me. I ran around and around him until the wind began to swirl into a tornado. Even a rhino couldn't escape that.

But an eagle could.

"DOUBLE UNFAIR!" I screamed.

Chance started dive-bombing me from the sky, trying to pick me up with his talons. I ran, somersaulted, and dodged him.

"ENOUGH!!" I yelled. "This is EXACTLY what Violet was talking about. We shouldn't be using our powers like this. And we're out in the open—do you want the whole world to see us?"

"Waaaahhh-waaaahhh-waaaahhh," Chance whined. "Why doesn't Baby Dash grow up and stop letting his sister do all his thinking for him?"

This was all getting out of hand at lightning speed.

◁ 🌸·🌸·🌸·🌸·🌸·🌸·🌸·🌸·🌸·🌸 ▷

You think? That's an understatement. Now let me finish the story, Dash.

So this was right about the point when I showed up looking for Dash. I hadn't been talking to him, but I was still keeping an eye on him. It wasn't like I was going to totally fail as a big sister—or as a Super.

"Home—NOW!" I yelled as I pointed my finger at Dash. "And you?" I said, turning to Chance. "You want to battle? Let's go!"

Chance turned back into a rhino and charged. But before he could reach me, I turned invisible and dodged him. He must not have expected that because he stopped and looked very confused. I used it to my advantage and surrounded him with a force field.

Chance turned back into himself. "You have powers, too???" he shouted. I guess Dash had kept his promise about not revealing our family secret. But I wasn't going to sit aside and watch this kid defeat my brother.

That was when Dash came running at ME! He stopped in his tracks, jumped up, and put his arms around me.

"I've got this, sis," he whispered in my ear. "I need to fight my own battles. And don't worry, I know you're right about Chance. I can take care of this."

I released Chance from my force field, even though my instincts told me not to. As I started to leave, I asked Dash to be careful. He might be annoying, but I knew I could trust him to do the right thing.

Come on, Vi. That's not what I did at all. I put my arms around you? Are you serious? And you know I would NEVER say that YOU'RE right.

Keep dreaming.

CHAPTER 11

DASH

Let me tell you the rest of the story.

As soon as I saw that Violet was out of sight, I turned back to Chance. I just stared at him.

"I'm done battling you," I told him. "Breaking into the office was wrong. I don't even want to know what kind of prank you had planned."

Chance listened quietly.

"Come on, Chance," I said. "That's not the kind of Super we want to be. That's not even Super. It's just wrong."

Chance's head dropped to his chest. He look defeated. "I know," he said. "It wasn't my plan. I'm not sure how I got so swept up in it."

I asked Chance whose plan it was. Then he told me a story that even I had a hard time believing at first. . . .

A few weeks ago, Chance began to really practice his powers. He started out at home by turning into his dog and his baby sister. He got bolder and tried it out at school. Then one day, he got a note in his locker. I taped it in here for further investigation:

I know who you are, Chance. And I know your secret. I have a mission that only you can accomplish. If you accept, respond to this note and put it back in your locker.

Chance thought one of his friends was playing a joke on him. Who leaves mysterious notes about secrets and missions in someone's locker? But he was curious, so he responded:

I don't know who you are, but I'm an open book! No secrets with me. Who is this? Greg? I'm guessing Greg. You think you're so hilarious.

The reply that Chance got was totally unexpected. I wouldn't have believed him if I hadn't seen the note for myself:

You are a Super. There's no shame in it. I'm a Super, too. If you're tired of hiding your true self, join me. I have a plan that will help Supers everywhere. It's our time to dominate!

I asked Chance how he knew that this person was a Super. It could've been anyone!

"At first, I thought it was a real Super, like Mr. Incredible or Elastigirl," Chance said. (HA! Mom and Dad would never do something like this. They don't even let _me_ do secret missions, let alone some kid they don't know.)

"Then I thought it was you when I first found out that you were a Super," Chance continued.

"That's why I pretended to be your sister and asked you all those questions. But you didn't seem to know anything about it."

The Super wanted to keep his (or her) identity a secret until he/she knew they could trust Chance. It was all starting to make sense, but I still didn't understand where the school records came into it. Chance explained that the mystery Super needed the records to expose an undercover super villain at the school. (I've been there, done that. There's no way a super villain is at school under MY watch. This Super must have been lying to Chance. I was starting to feel bad for him.)

"I thought I was doing a good thing," Chance explained. "I wanted to tell you, but the Super said I couldn't reveal the full plan to anyone. It was okay if a friend helped me, though."

"YOU TOLD THE SUPER ABOUT ME???"

I shouted.

"Not by name," said Chance. "I just said I met another Super who might be interested in helping the cause."

I was still pretty annoyed, but at least he didn't expose my secret identity. I asked Chance if he met the Super after he stole the records. That's when he looked really upset. He said the Super never showed up and still hadn't contacted him. I don't know who this person is, but he or she sounds terrible.

"That's why I didn't take the records very far," Chance added. "I hid them in one of the dumpsters in the parking lot until I figured out what to do. They were still there the last time I looked."

"Then it's time for a new plan," I told him as I looked up at the clock on the scoreboard. We had two minutes until the school doors would be locked for the night.

Chance thought we wouldn't make it.

Sigh . . .
everyone always
underestimates

THE DASH.

I told Chance to transform into something small. Here's how the next few minutes flew by:

4 seconds:
Chance (as a fly)
sat on my hand as
I zipped to the
dumpster.

8 seconds:
Chance (as a human)
dug through the
trash and started
to retrieve the
records.

9 seconds:
First trip. I picked up a stack, rushed through the school doors, and dashed to the main office.

12 seconds:
I put all the records back in place.

8 seconds:
I ran outside and started my second trip.

3 seconds:
I stopped for a drink of water—even THE DASH needs to stay hydrated.

8 seconds:
I put the records back in the file cabinet.

16 seconds:
I made my third and final trip with the last of the records.

3 seconds:
I zoomed out of the office and met up with Chance.

All done in **71** seconds!

That left **49** seconds to spare!

Don't tell anyone, but I've been working extra hard in math class lately.

Actually, you can tell Dad.

He'd like that.

After we returned the records, Chance and I just stood there.

It was really awkward.

I didn't know what to say, so I told him that I needed to get home—and I left.

Everything returned to normal at school. The teachers just thought it was some weird mystery about the disappearing (and reappearing) records—

Good thing they don't have a detective like me on the case!

I still haven't talked to Chance. He's avoiding me, but maybe that's for the best.

It was nice to have a Super friend,

at least for a little while. . . .

CHAPTER *12*
VIOLET

~~Dear Diary,~~
(Sorry, Diary, this one's for my brother.)

Dear Dash,

I just wanted to say . . .

I'm so proud of you.

I wasn't sure if you were going to rush into danger with Chance and forget everything Mom and Dad tried to teach us. But in the end, you were really Super.

WORLD'S
·BEST·
SUPER
BRO

DASH

I think it's time to talk to Chance. He made a bad decision, but that doesn't mean he's a bad kid. He thought he was doing something good. I think that mystery person was just using him. A good guy wouldn't make a kid steal stuff and then let him take the fall for it. This sounds more like a super villain!

I think Chance needs you now more than ever. You can show him what it means to be a Super—and keep a friend in the process.

That's why I know you won't mind that I invited him over to watch movies with us on Saturday night.

You did?

I just happened to be walking by his house after school the other day, and I saw him. He didn't think you'd want to talk to him again. But I told him how much you liked having him as a friend, so you would never hold a grudge. Especially since you've made your fair share of mistakes over the years!

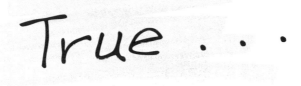

Saturday night was revealing. Once Dash and I got Chance alone, he apologized for everything. Over and over and over again. The kid was so sorry.

"I still don't know who left the notes,"
Chance said.

"Whoever it was, they promised that along with the pranks, we were going to help Supers all over the world. So I thought that even though it involved doing something bad, it would turn out to be good in the end. And it felt nice to be part of something big. I guess I got carried away. Now I know I shouldn't have let someone influence me. Especially someone I don't even know!"

"That's what I've been saying," I told Chance—and my brother. "I'm glad you finally realized it."

"I wouldn't have," Chance admitted. "If it weren't for Dash."

Dash smiled.

"Okay, Chance, are you ready to be initiated into the world of Parr family fun?"

"What's that?" Chance asked.

"Oh, you'll find out soon enough," I said as I rushed off to find Jack-Jack.

And then it was time for a Super skills challenge in the basement. Since Chance was the guest, he got to go first—and face off against Jack-Jack. He thought we were joking. Then he saw Jack-Jack turn into a red monster, and he knew we were very serious. Chance couldn't transform fast enough to escape the many powers of Jack-Jack.

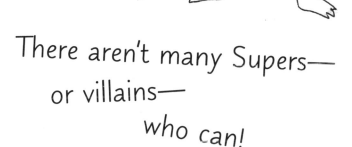

There aren't many Supers—
or villains—
who can!

Chance asked if we were all Supers. I think we can trust Chance with our family secret now, but that seemed like a story for another day. We'd need A LOT more time to explain all that.

See, we do make a good team, Vi. Just like I said. And I never thought I would say this . . . but maybe we should keep writing here. After all, we still need to figure out who was sending those notes to Chance. I want to solve THAT mystery. Are you in?

I am SUPER ready!

THE
END

Read the first chapter of

Super

Sleuths

now!

CHAPTER 1
VIOLET

Hi, Diary.
         I'm back.

But are you a "diary," really? I feel like you're more of a brother-sister-bonding therapy session or something. That just sounds sad and weird. We're supposed to be using the pages to solve a mystery, so maybe it's an Investigative Journal. <u>Super</u> Investigative Journal. Eh, what's in a name anyway. It doesn't matter.

So when we last wrote, Dash had a new best friend, Chance, who has shape-shifting Super powers and is a prankster like him. They goofed around and had a lot of fun, but Chance almost got into BIG trouble because of these creepy notes someone was leaving in his locker.

Some anonymous weirdo asked him to steal school records. Chance was going to do it because he believed it was going to be good for all Supers. He even tried to get Dash to help. Luckily, Dash wanted nothing to do with that prank, and Chance ended up realizing the whole thing was a mistake.

So now we're trying to figure out the identity of the creep who left those notes. I'll let Dash fill you in on the details. He and Chance are the lead detectives on this case—but I will tell you that we haven't figured it out yet. Chance hasn't received any other notes, so part of me wonders if we should let it go. I mean, maybe it was just some stupid kid pulling a prank on Dash and Chance. You know, someone getting back at them—giving them a dose of their own medicine.

It's more serious than that, Vi. Doesn't your gut tell you that? Or have you drifted so far into Normalville that you lost your sense of good and evil? Remember? The notes said he/she KNEW Chance was a Super and it was time to "dominate." That's no innocent prank!

I've been pretty busy at school, so I haven't had too much time to talk to Dash about it. I got stuck working on a massively boring presentation on the anatomy of plant cells with this kid in my class who does more grunting than talking. Gigi (my best friend) and I had planned to partner up, and then the teacher pulled the old "assigned partners" thing. I hate it when he does that. Sometimes I wonder if he can read my mind—how did he know to partner me up with the last person I would EVER choose? Maybe my science teacher is actually a super villain. . . . Now I'm starting to sound like Dash.

YES. I like the way you're thinking, Vi! If you need someone to investigate, you know where to find me.

So I created the model for our presentation AND I had to do the bulk of the presenting because my so-called partner left me stranded up there. (Can't say that was much of a surprise.)

I'm not sure if you know this about me yet, but I'm not a big fan of presentations. Public speaking is definitely NOT one of my Super powers. I'd take fighting a villain over speaking to a large group any day of the week. Unfortunately, that wasn't an option here. Thankfully, it's over. And I survived. Barely.

And you can probably guess why you haven't heard from Dash in a bit. He and Chance have been busy working on their powers. All. The. Time. If you ask me, I think they're a little obsessed. Mom and Dad don't really want us using our powers unless we really have to (they had no complaints when we helped rescue them from the Screenslaver, of course). For the most part, as far as daily life goes . . . they want us to just act like normal kids.

But we're NOT NORMAL KIDS!
We're AWESOME HEROES!

I know they wouldn't be happy if they found out how much time Dash has been practicing, but I'm not going to rat him out. He's been sparring with

Chance down in the basement at every opportunity. And since Dash is a trouble magnet, I'm thinking it may not be a bad thing for him to be safe at home with Chance.

You'll thank me the next time a super villain comes around—I will be MORE than ready for anything they throw at us.

I've been taking a little break from using my powers. I can't even remember the last time I used them. Oh, wait. Okay, so I did put Dash in a force field last night when he spilled popcorn all over my room and then tried to bolt before cleaning it up.

But other than that . . . Oh, wait. I also had to throw one around my cell model for science yesterday, when Jack-Jack was doing his laser-beam eye thingy. (There was NO WAY I was going to let him destroy my project—it took too long to make!)

I think that's just one of life's necessities when you have a baby brother with random powers that strike at any moment. Now that I think about it, I probably use my powers against the ~~evil~~ forces of brothers more than anything else! *awesome*

I've been hanging out with Gigi a lot, too—but I can't use my powers in front of her. For all she knows, I'm completely normal. And that's the way I have to keep it. Normal has actually been fun, though.

normal = boring

I mean, sure, it <u>is</u> a little weird not being able to tell my best friend that I'm able to vanish into thin air or create nearly indestructible force fields, but . . . well, it is what it is. I guess it's extra weird because her uncle is Frozone. It'd be awesome if she knew about him.

I actually have no idea if she's aware of her uncle's powers. If she knew about him, then maybe I could tell her about me and my powers. Every now and then, she makes a comment when his name comes up that makes me wonder if she knows. Like the other day, when she told me she couldn't go to the movies, she said, "Uncle Lucius is coming by to take me and my little sister out for frozen yogurt." And when she said "frozen," she kind of looked at me in a weird way. I wanted to ask her SOOO bad. But I didn't. If she doesn't know about his secret life as a Super, I'd mess everything up for him. And I definitely do not want to (and CANNOT) do that. We all know—

 our identity is our most valuable possession

(as Mom likes to tell us ten million times a day), so I definitely have to keep my mouth shut.

At the moment, the best thing to do is just focus on my normal side and enjoy doing normal stuff with my normal best friend—

I'm cool with that.

Speaking of normal . . .

I have some news. The rec center is starting up this new after-school program. I guess they're going to have different activities—sports, arts and crafts, games, stuff like that. My parents signed Dash and me up! They keep telling us we need to be "well-rounded," and of course, they're all about getting us involved in normal activities. Typically, I wouldn't be too thrilled about it, but Gigi's parents signed her up, too, so I know it will be fun. We're going to do **EVERYTHING** together. I'm kind of excited because it'll be great to get some extra time with her every day.

Continue to read the next

VIOLET & DASH

adventure in:

Super Sleuths